Dedicated to all the little creatures in my life.

Including and especially Mark.

LITTLE BIRDS OF A FEATHER

The Fantastic Adventures of Steve & Timmy

A True Story by Nanette Kryske Towsley

Once upon a time . . .

Hey wait a minute, this is a true story, not some fairy tale.
It wasn't all that long ago either. There is a giant cactus in my
front yard. This saguaro cactus is probably over 200 years
old—although I have only lived in my home for about twenty years.
Most cactus specialists know how to calculate the age of saguaro
from the number and size of the arms.

This cactus was riddled with holes made by the local birds during
their nesting time each spring. Cactus wrens, woodpeckers,
starlings, lovebirds, sparrows, grackles, and even a few parakeets
found refuge in these customized bird apartments throughout
the big arms of this cactus.

The year in question, 2009, was no different from any other. Anyone walking down the street could hear the chirping and cheeping from all the baby birds growing up in their little nests. Sometimes baby birds would fall out of their nests—during a windstorm, or by stepping too close to the edge of the hole.

Yikes! And that is where this story begins: with two little baby birds who happened to fall out and make their way onto my front porch.

6

Can you count the number of arms
on this cactus?

One morning on the way to work, I walked out the front door
and headed to the car. There was a tiny little black and grey
blob with big yellow lips looking up at me from the rocks in
the garden. It was making a sweet little sound. I knew it was
alive. Many of the baby birds that fall great distances die.

But this little bird, not only survived the fall from the
nest, but found his way into my path. I got down to his
level very slowly and gently and put my hand out.
The little bird jumped into my palm. "Phew!" he must
have been thinking, "Found someone to help me get
back to the nest."

Well, that wasn't going to be the case since the saguaro
was way too tall and too spiny. I had no idea which nest
he fell from. There were so many holes to choose from.
And besides, I knew once a baby bird is touched by a
human, the mother bird won't care for them anymore.

Well, just for the record, all my research shows this is hogwash.
According to Snopes.com:

Mother birds will not reject their babies
because they smell human scent on them, nor will
they refuse to sit on eggs that have been handled by
a person. Most birds have a limited sense of smell
and cannot detect human scent. (If you handle bird
eggs while the mother is away from the nest, mama
bird will usually notice upon her return that the
eggs were disturbed during her absence, and some
species of bird will take this as an indication that
a dangerous intruder is present and may temporarily
or even permanently abandon their nests as a result.
Such behavior is relatively rare, however, and in
these situations the mother birds are reacting to
visual warnings, not
olfactory ones.)

This was my introduction to Steve. I picked him up and put him in a shoe box I dug out of the garage for just such occasions. I stuffed the box with soft paper towels, grabbed an eye dropper, and made my way to the office to continue my new "mama" duties from the office—after a brief pit-stop to the pet store for some baby bird formula.

Meanwhile, while I was driving, my husband, Mark, went out to get the newspaper, when low and behold on the front porch was another baby bird just like the one I had found. In an instant, my cell phone rang and on the other end, was a panicked voice, "Guess what Honey? I found a baby bird on the front porch! How fast can you come home and help me get him?"

And so we were introduced to Timmy.

I back-tracked around, picked up the new passenger, and headed back   to the office with both birdies, an eye dropper, and baby formula in hand. And a new adventure was about to begin.

14

Since there were two, I quickly located a small parakeet cage
I had and set up shop for the new friends. The little boys had
voracious (really big) appetites and screeched for their new
human slave to feed them hourly.

I discovered a special formula several years ago when I rescued
a baby woodpecker who fell from the exact same cactus. Some
people soak cat or dog food in a little water to make a mush that
can be pushed through an eye dropper. That works also, but the
Lafeber's Instant Nutri-Start Baby Bird Formula is specially-made
for the youngest of birds.

This is the stuff. Just mix it
with a little water and make
it any consistency you'd like.

The baby-babies like it runny,
but as they get older they
like it goopier, like cake.
You still need to give them
water, very carefully.

The special bird formula was nutritionally good for the boys, and they liked the taste. They could not get enough.

Sometimes I had to hold them when I fed them. They were just too cute. But since I had to deal with two little ones at once, it was easier to snatch and grab one at a time and feed them individually. I knew I wanted to let them go free but I felt they would overcome their human contact in time, as they were weaned from food and human attention.

For weeks, Steve and Timmy came to work with me in their little cage since they were still eating every hour or two. They got very used to the car ride and actually looked forward to all the sights and sounds of the drive and the office. Each afternoon they came home with me and found their special spot on top of the washer and dryer. It was high enough away from the many dogs who had also decided to make me their human slave and companion.

These were the four lazy dogs.
No, that is not a "coffee table."
That is a wooden dog bed.

Our household was constantly blessed with lots of creatures:
from the newly found baby birds to several dogs, several cats,
a couple of cockatoos, a handful of fish, and down the street,
a horse.

This is Woody, the Wonder Horse!

As time went on, Steve and Timmy continued to grow and chirp—
ever more loudly. They became very accustomed to their routine
and all the new humans and animals in their life.

The boys still needed lessons in how to eat on their own, and fend for themselves in the real world (the outside world of birds). The next step was to change their diet to include bugs and meal worms to be more like the natural environment. They also needed to learn about how to find water to drink. I did my best "mama bird" impressions, but it was just going to take some time for them to mature. And, I wasn't going to demonstrate (show them) how to eat worms.

Who you looking at?
I've got a "big boy" beak now.

In a matter of weeks to months, or 15 cans of mealworms later, the boys were "getting it."

Steve and Timmy still came to my office but didn't need to eat as frequently, and now I could put the worms on the bottom of their cage and they would hop down and pick them up with their beaks. Their beaks ceased to be the bright yellow color they once were. Now, they were growing up to be "big boys" and were right on track for their normal course of development.

In the office, away from all the home critters, I let the boys fly a bit to get a sense of their wings. They took to that like a fish takes to water. I guess that is what Ma Nature had in mind for all her creatures.

Hey, it's lonely up here!
Shut up! At least we have a tree house.

Next step for Steve and Timmy: acclimating (getting used to) to the outside environment while still being protected from all the elements. My brilliant idea of the day was to create a tree house for the boys with a larger cage bungee-corded into a big tree. You can create just about anything you want with bungee cords and duct tape. (I think I could even build a house to live in. But that is a story for another time.)

So up they went into the big Mulberry tree on the side of our house.

While the cage looked so small compared to the tree,
it was quite a bit larger than the little cage they
were living in previously. Now, they could hear all of
the other birds and the sights and sounds of the real
outside world, but still be safe from predators
as they got used to their future.

26

Also, they got more flying practice—very important stuff at this stage. I put worms in the cage before work and when I came home in the late afternoon. They had fresh water in a couple of bowls inside the cage. Not sure whether it was Steve or Timmy, or both, but someone found the drinking water a perfect place to take a birdie bath. All a part of their learning process for the next leg of their journey. They lived in this cage for about 7 days and I decided it was time to open the door and let them explore.

If they flew away it was time, if it wasn't they would still have the cage to call home. But it needed to be up to them. And so the big day came.

I opened the door . . .

And at first, they sat there. Or to be technically
correct, they stood there—staring at me, like what's the
big deal. Bring on the worms. Then with a gentle grab, I
helped them out of the door. They immediately took to
flight. Yes, I was a bit sad, but happy that they would
have a chance to go be "their own birdies" now. Or so I
thought. They flew immediately to the neighbor's roof.
Walked around a bit. Then flew back to the block wall
between our homes and stood there screaming for their
next meal—kind of like   homing pigeons but by now, we
knew that Steve and Timmy were starlings.

That's me!
No, that's me, silly!
Where are we?

And so it went for almost two and a half months,
both boys would cruise around, never staying in their
makeshift tree house again, but hanging in the
neighboring trees. They would hear me in the
backyard and scream to me. Or I would call them
by name as if I were calling some little undisciplined
children: "Steevee, Timmy, yoo hoo, boys, where
are you?" And they would come flying to a certain
spot on the block wall and wait for me to dump out
the day's selection of mealworms. At first, they
came around two to three times a day. Progressively
as time went on, they came only once-a-day.

Check it out, a wild
birdie in the tree.
No, it's Steve!

One day, I was driving with my car windows down
enjoying the beautiful Arizona spring we were
having, and I heard the boys calling to me from
almost a mile away. By the time I pulled into the
driveway, there they were hovering in the neighbors
trees screaming for me to hurry with the worms.
While I was very honored that they could still love
a human, I wanted them to be able to be free as
they were intended to be. Changes were taking place.
Even though they came for food, they resisted me
holding or petting them. And so I didn't press the
issue anymore. I wanted them to feel free to move
on when nature called them.

34

Soon, only one bird, Timmy, was coming back for his daily meal. Steve had obviously found a new life or a companion. At first I was worried and combed the property, assuming the worst. But no, he was doing what he needed to do.

A few weeks later, Timmy, too, disappeared to his own world. Many grown-up starlings come to visit—because they all grew up in the big cactus out front. They all looked like the boys, so I'm not sure anymore if Steve and Timmy are among them. In fact, I'm not even sure that Steve and Timmy were boys. They perhaps could have been little girl birds and maybe started families of their own.

This is not a sad story, but a very happy one.

It is about learning to care for another one of God's
creatures. It suggests that research and investigation can
lead you to good information to do the right things. It is also
about understanding the natural order of things, and knowing
when it is time to let go.

It is not really any different than letting go of our own
children into the world. While it is a wild and sometimes
dangerous place, it is also a place where the right beginnings
lead to happy and fulfilling lives as they were intended to be.

Boy,
this is sure
fun!

Each day when the birds gather in the cactus out front
of my home, I look to see if Steve and Timmy have
come home to roost and have babies of their own.

But wherever they are, I know I helped them in their time of need, and beyond all measure, they helped and taught me as well. You can't ask for much more than that.

Guess it's
time to move
on . . .

And so history repeats itself:

Meet Greenbird the love Bird.

And meet Pickles the Dove.

and Eggbert
the Grackle.

43

They were all rescued from
the same place.

And so it goes.
Everyone lived happily ever after.

The End.

or is it really?